This book belongs to

_____

Barbie

in

The Ice Dragon

Illustrations by
Pam Duarte and Allan Choi

EGMONT

EGMONT

We bring stories to life

First published in Great Britain 2007
By Egmont UK Limited
239 Kensington High Street, London W8 6SA

BARBIE and associated trademarks and trade dress are owned by,
and used under license from, Mattel, Inc.
© 2007 Mattel, Inc.

ISBN 978 1 4052 3107 7

1 3 5 7 9 10 8 6 4 2

Printed in Germany

Hello! My name is Aurora and I am the Sky Goddess.

This is the story of what happened when the wicked goddess, Ethereal, stole the weather key . . .

High in Cloud Kingdom in a beautiful Cloud Castle lived Aurora, the Sky Goddess. She was the protector of Cloud Kingdom and it was her duty to ensure that no harm came to this beautiful, enchanted land.

Aurora had many magical friends who also lived in the Cloud Castle, and whenever Aurora needed their help, they were always at her side.

One bright, cold morning, Kosmo, Aurora's kestrel friend, flew through her window in a panic.

"Aurora," he cried, "you have to help. Spring has disappeared and the seasons have not changed."

"Wherever can Spring be?" Aurora wondered anxiously. "This is her busiest time of year. Normally, she'd be waking the flowers and telling the trees to blossom. Come on, Kosmo, we should try to find her."

At the enchanted glade where the Season Sprites lived, Aurora and Kosmo found Spring crying on Winter's shoulder.

"The wicked goddess, Ethereal, has stolen our weather key," Spring told the friends, "and we can't change the seasons. If we don't change them soon it will be winter forever!"

"Don't worry," said Aurora. "I'll get your weather key back! Kosmo, you and I must go to Ethereal's palace at once."

In her cold, dark tower, Ethereal looked into her crystal ball. As the swirling crystals settled, she saw Aurora.

"Ha!" she scoffed to herself. "So you think you can come here and just ask for the weather key?

I have bigger plans for you than that – I want the Element Diamond and you are just the person to get it for me!"

Aurora walked bravely in to Ethereal's tower.

"Please may I have the weather key back?" she pleaded with the wicked goddess. "Without it, spring cannot come to Cloud Kingdom."

"You may have it back," Ethereal replied, "but only if you bring me the Element Diamond from the Ice Dragon who lives at Glass Mountain, on the far side of the Kingdom. But you had better be careful – the Dragon can command the snow and freeze you with a single stare."

Aurora left the tower. "Why does Ethereal want the Element Diamond?" she wondered.

With a whistle, Aurora summoned the Four Winds – beautiful horses that could run as fast as the wind. They were pulling a magnificent shining sleigh.

"Can you take me to Glass Mountain?" asked Aurora, stroking each horse in turn.

The Four Winds agreed, and with Aurora aboard the sleigh, they took off, leaving a trail across the clouds.

After a long journey, Aurora finally saw the peaks of Glass Mountain glittering in the distance. But before it, lay the Sea of Mirrors. As soon as the horses' hooves touched the shining surface, it started to crack and splinter.

"How are we going to cross the Sea?" Aurora asked the Four Winds as she picked up a piece of the cracked mirror.

Suddenly, a pair of Rainbow Archers appeared and, drawing their bows, they shot rainbow arrows across the Sea of Mirrors to create a colourful bridge for Aurora and her friends to safely cross.

But the friends' peril was not yet over. As they neared Glass Mountain, a terrible blizzard blew up around them. The snowflakes stung their skin.

"The Ice Dragon must have heard us coming and sent a blizzard to stop us," squawked Kosmo. But the Four Winds' warm breath blew at the blizzard and pushed it away.

When finally they reached the mountain, Aurora couldn't find a way into the Ice Dragon's den. The Dragon had sealed the entrance with a huge rock of crystal.

"What are we going to do?" asked Kosmo.

Aurora clapped her hands and summoned a thunderbolt from the sky, which cracked the rock in front of them with a loud bang.

Behind the rock was an icy maze within a sparkling grotto. In the ceiling, tiny jewels shone like stars and icicles like frosty fingers hung down about them.

"Kosmo," Aurora told her friend, "gather as many jewels as you can in your beak. We will use them to lay a trail so we can find our way out again."

At the centre of the icy maze sat the Ice Dragon. Around his neck hung the Element Diamond.

"Who dares to enter my cave?" roared the Dragon as he turned towards Aurora, his eyes blazing with fire and ice.

Remembering Ethereal's words, Aurora held up the piece of broken mirror from the Sea of Mirrors. The Dragon's freezing stare reflected back at him and he was turned to a statue of ice.

Aurora snatched the diamond from the Dragon's neck and fled, following Kosmo's gemstone trail.

Aurora took the diamond to Ethereal as quickly as she could.

"With this diamond I can summon the Four Elements – Earth, Air, Fire and Water – and rule Cloud Kingdom," Ethereal told Aurora.

But the Element Diamond could only be held by one with a pure heart. In Ethereal's grasp it shone brightly, wrapping the wicked goddess in light. With a blinding flash, she disappeared, as the diamond flew from her hand.

As Aurora caught the diamond, it glowed softly. Gradually, the Water Element appeared from the gem, accompanied by Earth, Air and Fire.

"We would like you to be our new protector," the Elements asked Aurora, who gladly agreed.

Kosmo returned the weather key to the Season Sprites, and they watched in delight as the flowers began to wake, and the trees to blossom.

Spring had returned to Cloud Kingdom at last, and Aurora and her friends celebrated amongst the trees.